To my husband **KENNETH TURNER** and son **CHRISTIAN TURNER**, your support has never wavered. Thanks for the continued encouragement.

www.mascotbooks.com

Rex's Journey: Helping Children Understand and Cope With Emotions

For more information, please contact:
Mascot Books
620 Herndon Parkway, Suite 320
Herndon, VA 20170
info@mascotbooks.com

Library of Congress Control Number: 2017917386

CPSIA Code: PRT0318A
ISBN-13: 978-1-68401-570-2

Printed in the United States

REX'S JOURNEY

HELPING CHILDREN UNDERSTAND AND COPE WITH EMOTIONS

Written by
Dr. Ambroes Pass-Turner

Illustrated by
Agus Prajogo

Rex was a happy
six-year-old boy who
lived with his father, mother,
brother, and sister. His sister Roxie
was his best friend.

They played ball and chased each
other around the backyard all the
time. Rex enjoyed going to school,
he made good grades, and got
along well with his friends.

But one day, Rex's attitude changed. Instead of being happy and fun, he would feel sad and angry for no reason. Rex didn't understand why this happened. This made him feel like he had no control over his emotions.

When he was sad and angry, he didn't want to play with his sister Roxie or follow the rules at home, like putting the toys back in the toy box.

At school, he didn't listen to the teacher. Instead, he fought with others and ignored his classwork. Soon, his grades began to fall, and he had to spend his recess completing classroom work. Once, he threw a basketball at his friend and was placed in time out. Rex's friends didn't want to play with him anymore because of his actions. They were afraid he would throw a basketball at them as well. This made Rex even more angry and sad.

Rex's behavior was so bad that he was sent to see the principal, Mr. Cloud. He called Rex's parents and told them that maybe Rex should see a counselor. Mr. Cloud gave them a list of counselors in the area who could help Rex.

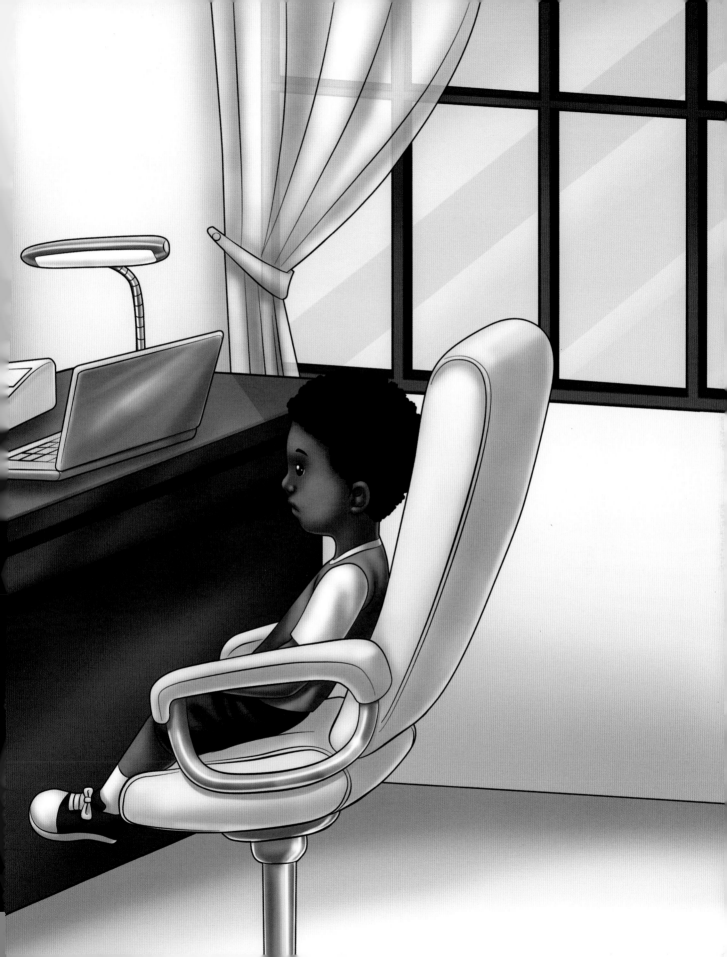

Rex was afraid to go see a counselor, but his parents said they would go with him, so he felt much better about going. Dad, Mom, and Rex went to counselor Mr. Brown's office. The office was full of bright colors and had a big toy box filled with lots of toys!

Rex played with the firetruck while his mom and dad talked with the counselor.

Then, his parents left the room, so Rex and Mr. Brown could talk. Rex was afraid, but the counselor had a table with toys, crayons, construction paper, and books, so he wasn't that afraid.

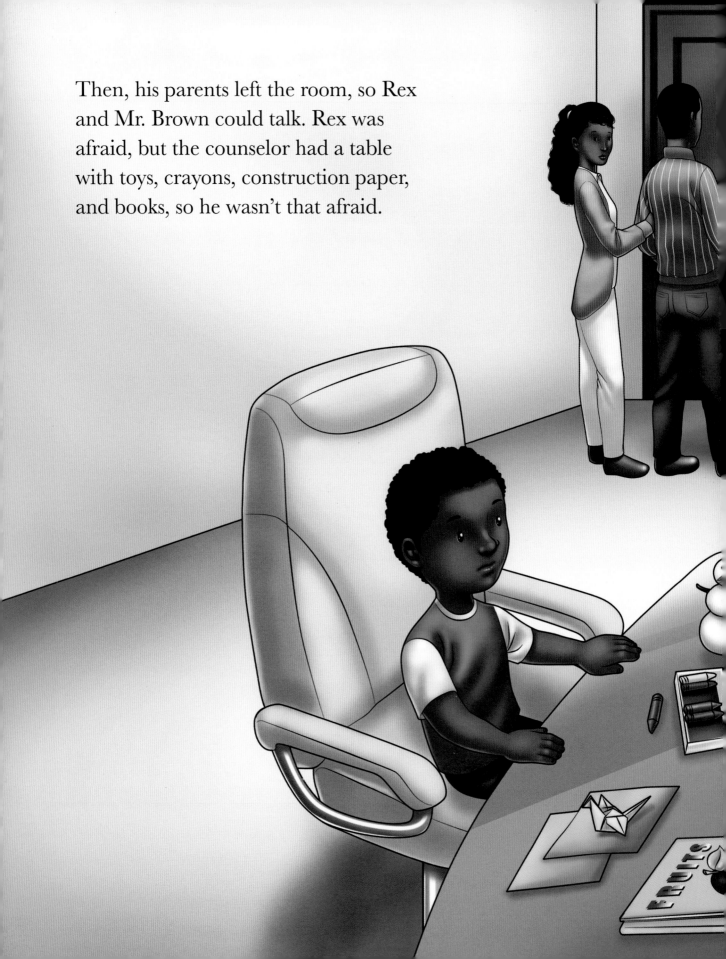

Mr. Brown asked him about school, and Rex said he was sad about how the students bullied him and how no one would play with him.

Mr. Brown suggested that when Rex felt angry or sad, he do an activity that made him happy. Rex said he liked drawing and coloring, so his counselor asked him to draw a picture of his family.

Rex drew a picture of him and his sister Roxie playing outside while his parents watched from the kitchen window. It made him think about how his father would take him bike riding and his mom would watch cartoons with him, and he felt less angry and sad.

Mr. Brown encouraged Rex to keep drawing and coloring when he felt sad. He told Rex to try and spend thirty minutes a week on an activity he enjoyed.

Mr. Brown also taught Rex how to take deep breaths to calm himself down when he felt angry. He told Rex to imagine blowing out the candles on his birthday cake. Another way to calm himself down is to listen to his inside voice and count to 10.

When he felt sad, Mr. Brown told Rex it was OK to reach out and talk with parents, teachers, his school counselor, or a friend.

Rex practiced his healthy coping skills whenever he felt angry and sad. He took deep breaths, counted to 10, did activities he enjoyed, and talked with his parents, teachers, counselors, and friends.

As time went on,
he began to feel less
angry and sad, and he
found he could control his emotions and negative behavior. Dad and
Mom spent special time with Rex weekly, and his friends allowed him to
play with them again. Soon, Rex was a happy and fun kid again.

ABOUT THE AUTHOR

Dr. Ambroes Pass-Turner is a Doctor of Counseling Psychology and founder of APT Counseling Services, LLC. She is a professor and author. Dr. Pass-Turner published the book *Childhood Sexual Abuse: Pathway to Mental Health Issues and Delinquent Behavior*. She has served as a subject matter expert on the topics "Why some survivors minimize their abuse: When this coping mechanism can be a good thing," and "How survivors' advocates can avoid burnout" with national publication agency Domestic Shelters. Dr. Pass-Turner is an expert in working with behavioral and emotionally disturbed children, adults, families, and offenders within the criminal justice system. She conducts professional seminars and workshops that focus on empowerment, enhancing professional development, and life skills. Dr. Pass-Turner obtained a Doctor of Education in Counseling Psychology from the College of Behavioral Sciences at Argosy University. She earned a Master of Science in Counseling and Human Development, and a Bachelor of Science in Human Services with a double minor in psychology and sociology from Troy State University. Dr. Pass-Turner holds credentials as a Licensed Professional Counselor, Board Certified Professional Counselor, National Certified Counselor, Certified Clinical Mental Health Counselor, Clinically Certified Domestic Violence Counselor, and Clinically Certified Forensic Counselor with a specialty in child custody evaluation and forensic assessment/evaluation. She is a member of the American Psychological Association, American Psychotherapy Association, National Board for Certified Counselors, National Association of Forensic Counselors, and Delta Sigma Theta Sorority, Inc.

Have a book idea?
Contact us at:

info@mascotbooks.com | www.mascotbooks.com